The Virtues,
the Vices and
All the Passions

Anita Phillips

CW00551881

Polygon
EDINBURGH

© Anita Phillips 1991
First published by
Polygon
22 George Square, Edinburgh

Set in Linotron Sabon
by Koinonia, Bury and
Printed and bound in
Great Britain by
Redwood Press, Melksham, Wiltshire

British Library Cataloguing in
Publication Data
Phillips, Anita
    The virtues, the vices and all the passions
    I. Title
    823'.914 [F]

ISBN 0 7486 6092 7

The publisher acknowledges subsidy
from the Scottish Arts Council
towards the publication of this volume

Contents

For Olivier Richon

ICONOLOGIE

VELOCITE.

C'eſt la rapidité du mouvement, caractériſée par
une femme qui lance une fleche, & qui eſt en
action de courir, ayant des aîles au dos, & des ta-
lonnieres ſemblables à celles de Mercure, deſquelles
Virgile dit:

> *Et primum pedibus talaria nectit*
> *Aurea: quæ ſublimem alis, ſive æquora ſupra,*
> *Seu terram rapido pariter cum flamine portant.*

SPEED

This is rapidity of movement, characterised by a woman who throws an arrow, and is in the action of running, having wings upon her back and winged heels similar to those of Mercury, of which Virgil says:

> ... *Et primum pedibus talaria nectit*
> *Aurea: quae sublimem alis, sive aequora supra,*
> *Seu terram rapido pariter cum flamine portant.*

Vira was driving an old car, a black Citroën, belonging to her friend Dora. Eyes flickering in the mirror, checking the traffic behind. She turned the steering wheel and moved out onto the main road. Romantic music, a Brahms piano concerto, played very loud.

She was driving this old car along a main road which cut the open country. For a long time there was nothing but the feeling of moving forward, without the landscape changing.

The landscape remained the same.

The music continued.

The car moved forward.

This feeling lasted for some time. Then, with a click, the tape switched off. Vira didn't take out the tape and insert another. She let the sound of the engine and the air rushing past the car take the place of Brahms.

The landscape remained the same.

The car moved forward.

The car in front of Vira's, an ancient British make, unaccountably swerved onto the embankment and braked to a halt. Vira braked magnificently to avoid its tail. The seat-belt saved her from a dive through the windscreen. Her eyes opened wide and then closed completely. Luckily, there was nothing behind. She sat still.

A hedgehog had been granted an extended lease of life. It crept across the road, already an old hedgehog, a bit out of breath and puzzled in its mind.

The man from the car in front came over to Vira and apologised for swerving in such a dangerous way. Vira opened her eyes to look at him. She didn't open her pale lips. As a child I was often car-sick.

- I am sorry. I suppose I'm sentimental. I can't bear to see the squashed ones. You don't share my feeling?

Vira found that in an emergency, her fingers could unfasten the seat-belt - something miraculous, like God's grace; and that she had just the strength to stretch over to the passenger door, push it open, lean over and abandon herself to an attack of vomiting, half-kneeling and half-crouching on the seats.

Gradually the convulsions of anti-peristalsis changed into a fit of sobbing which made her sound like a small, sad, chained-up dog. She struggled upright and grabbed for the tissues to swab her face, which had a dismal, shattered look.

The man was now sitting in the driving seat, looking anxious and holding a bottle of mineral water.

- I thought you might like some of this. To take the bad taste away.

She rinsed her mouth with the water and spat it out in the same direction as the vomit, then closed the door. She drank some.

- You can keep the bottle.

- Thank you, said Vira ironically. He didn't seem to notice the irony.

- I feel marginally better, she added.

- Good. I'm terribly sorry.

- Actually, I still feel awful.

- Perhaps you'd better rest here until you feel better.

- Yes. You go on, though. I'll be all right in a minute.

- Don't worry. I'm not in a hurry.

Vira and the man sat in silence for some time. Occasionally she sipped from the bottle. In this way, the chemical constitution of her insides gradually returned to normal.

- I bet you prefer animals to humans, don't you? she said with a return of strength. Later, when she found out that the man's name was Angel, it seemed to have been appropriate to have recognised something not quite human about him, despite his voice, teeth, hair and other superficial human attributes. But at this point I had no idea that I would ever meet him again.

- That depends, he replied as if the question did not interest him.

He did not seem at all the sort of person that Vira would ever meet again. He wore a Fair Isle sweater and had no particular accent.

- Well, I'm all right except for a blotchy face, said Vira. She then started to cry again. Why was it that I started to cry again? She did this because she liked to do certain things more than once. She could enjoy the second time as she could not have enjoyed the first.

FRANCOISE.

CONTAGION.

Infection dangereufe, qui fe répand des chofes corrompues fur les chofes faines, & par laquelle la corruption fe communique. Elle fe repréfente par une femme pâle, exténuée, & vêtue d'habits fales & déchirés, pour dénoter les affreufes miferes qui l'accompagnent. Elle tient une branche de noyer & s'appuye fur un bafilic, animal dont le foufle & le regard font contagieux, felon quelques auteurs. L'adolefcent moribond qui eft couché à fes piés, & la vapeur épaiffe qui l'environne, défignent l'infection de l'air.

H 3

CONTAGION

A dangerous infection which spreads
corruption to healthy things, and by
which corruption is passed on. It is
represented by a pale, exhausted
woman dressed in dirty, torn clothing to denote the terrible distress
which accompanies contagion. She is
holding a walnut branch and leaning
against a basilisk, an animal whose
breath and look are contagious,
according to certain authors. The
dying youth lying at her feet, and the
thick haze which surrounds her,
indicate the infection of the air.

Not only the tears, but the sickness came back too. Things repeated themselves, changing from natural to supernatural phenomena.

I had gone out for company. It was late and I had reached the pavement, detached from the group I had been with, when my stomach sharply contracted with pain. I crouched down on the pavement, in a foetal position. A middle-aged woman crossed the road, wanting to know if I was well. I didn't want to answer her but nor did I want to be rude. I fashioned a smile by stretching my lips out at each edge. She walked on immediately.

I was able to stand up, eventually, and as I put my hand out to smooth my hair. I touched a layer of stickiness on my forehead.

I'm ill. Inexplicably the previous day's events had triggered the illness. I'm impaled on the hedgehog's spikes. Gypsies roast hedgehogs and eat them. Several taxis passed me with their lights on, taking me for a drunk. I wish I could telephone Dora. Dora would be the one to rescue me. But this time she couldn't.

When I reached her place, my head was aching, and under the arms. The room's dark, the cur-

21

tains closed. I lay under the covers. The covers are suffocating. The darkness went. The room surrounds me, not as close as the dark. I was on my own in the big house. I felt I was lying in a pool of my own sweat.

It must be a fever. I wish I could stop shivering. It's not cold. Actually, I'm hot. If I looked in the bathroom mirror, my eye-whites would be yellow. I'm sure they would be.

Maybe I'm changing irrevocably. Perhaps my hair will have turned white. Perhaps I'll have lost weight, that would be good.

Dora would know what to do, if she were here. I'm glad she's away. Always holding onto Dora. She knows what to do, always. I'm glad she's away.

I can't do anything. What do I want to do? Read something. But nothing's impossible. Why did I take out the car the other day? Because of looking. The landscape goes past like an endless film with no narrative. It just goes past. Doesn't bother you with too many meanings. Yes, I liked that.

That man, Angel.

I wish Dora wouldn't come back. I've nothing to show her.

I wish she was here, now.

The room darkened again.

ICONOLOGIE

DESIR

en général.

Il fe repréfente fous la figure d'une jeune fille pref-
que nue, parce que c'eft dans cet âge que l'on
eft plus porté à defirer. La flamme qui lui fort de
la tête & les ailes qu'elle a aux tempes, dénotent
fon ardeur & fa vélocité. Elle s'occupe à confidérer
divers objets idéals, qui font indiqués par un amour
tenant un portrait ou un chiffre orné de fleurs: par
un trophée d'armes, & une piramide. Ces objets la
détournent des bijoux qu'elle poffede & qui font près
d'elle.

DESIRE

It is represented by a young woman, nearly naked, because it is at this age that one is most carried away by desire. The flame which comes from her head and the wings at her temples signify the swiftness and intensity of desire. She is looking at various ideal objects, denoted by a cupid holding a portrait or a figure decorated with flowers, a military trophy and a pyramid. These objects distract her from the jewels which she owns and which are close to her.

Three days of sweating had taken all the weight out of her. She was feeling light in the frame, mobile. Looking from the doorway into the room, she could have been at a Parisian salon of the twenties: Turkish carpets, drifting cigarette smoke, pools of light gilding clothes. And Dora coming towards her to embrace her. The scent of some infinitely distilled essence originating in a long-dead flower or harmless animal. Vira taken and dispensed with a single theatrical gesture, already grasping at the memory of softness.

- Vira! she said, looking away towards a young man at the window. Well, what have you been doing while I've been away?

- I've been lying in bed upstairs. I've been ill.

Dora made some sort of noise which illustrated an absence of interest.

I can't even remember how I met her; certainly not how she became more and more a permanent fixture to the extent that I find myself living here. After a month away, you'd think she'd be happier to see me. She's bored, I suppose. So am I. A bored symbiosis.

Vira was taken to a man in a dark suit. A sullen face. He reminds me of no-one else. He seems to absorb light. Dora said it was strange that we had never met before. I don't see why. This is Fell, she said. Then she went off in a straight line for the window.

Fell and Vira were exactly the same height. Fell didn't smile much, but didn't lose anything by it. Later in the evening, when he did smile, or rather laugh, he showed shark's teeth and a red flash of tongue. Red muscular tongue under crooked, shark teeth. Sharks are excited by the smell of blood.

Vira let him talk, which he did well, with a varied selection of tones and subjects which followed seamlessly one after the next. She was serious, especially when he knew dates and times and was not afraid to quote them. He demanded only her collusion and her indulgence. She didn't mind giving these things in return for his eyes remaining fixed on her face, as they did. Perhaps I should have listened a little more closely. It might have helped me.

Whenever he moved his eyes away from her, she thought she would rise in the air from the tension of waiting until they would return. She needed to fix herself into place with his look, to allow him to subsume her completely. It had happened almost immediately.

He went to find drinks. She quickly looked around the room. Dora had the young man by the arm; his colour was high. People were in groups or couples, and through the French windows the foliage shook violently and scratched against the glass.

She watched Fell. His return was blocked by a woman in blue who had an urgent posture. Vira's lips pressed together. She had formed a conscious intention of leaving with him. She was holding onto herself until he came back.

FRANÇOISE.

VOLUPTE.

C'est un excès qui tient de la moleffe, & du liberti-
nage. Il ne convient qu'aux grands, & aux ri-
ches, par les dépenfes exceffives qu'il occafione.

On le perfonnifie fous la figure d'une belle femme
dont les joues font colorées du plus vif incarnat. Ses
regards font languiffants, & fon attitude lafcive. Elle
eft couchée fur un lit de fleurs, & tient une boule de
verre qui a des aîles. Ce hiéroglyphe fignifie que les
plaifirs de la terre, tels voluptueux qu'il foient, font
momentanés, & paffent auffi promptement qu'ils fe
goutent.

SENSUAL PLEASURE

This is an excess which runs to
indolence and licentiousness. It
applies only to the great and the
rich, through their excessive ex-
penditure.

It is personified by the figure of a
beautiful woman whose cheeks are
coloured the brightest rose pink. She
has a languishing look and a lascivi-
ous pose. She lies on a bed of flowers and holds a glass sphere which
has wings. This hieroglyph signifies
that earthly pleasures, however
voluptuous, are temporary and pass
as soon as they are tasted.

- The heat in here ...

- Would you like to sit down? he asked.

- No. I won't stay here much longer.

- I shall be going soon, myself.

- Are you tired?

- No, I'm not tired.

I laughed quietly. He did not smile, refusing the dullness of quick collusion, prolonging the game. I began to feel a sense of urgency. Perhaps that is what he wants. I want to move towards or away from him. I was terrified that I was mistaken about my interpretation of his words and gestures. But I was confident of not showing my terror, or my interpretation.

I headed for the bathroom. The first thing I did was to look at myself in the mirror. My face was flushed and my eyes very bright, transparently lustful and eager. I splashed my face with cold water and dabbed it with one of Dora's towels. I combed my hair and adjusted my clothing. I made a decision.

He was still alone when I came out to find him. I looked straight at him, my face heating again on entering the room. We could talk, or I could say what it was, listening to him hearing it.

- I need some air, I said. I need to get out of here.

Now is the difficult part. I waited for a moment, but he didn't speak.

- I can borrow one of Dora's cars, I said.

- Or you could come out in mine, he said finally, looking away at the woman in blue. Then he looked back at me and smiled slightly.

- I'm going now.

He drove silently along the river bank, where homeless men live, past the mediterranean-style restaurant terraces and the old, still riverboats.

The speed of movement, like the smooth flexing of a man's arm.

We entered the deserted area at the far east of the city, the edge of the docklands. Unused now and all along the docks loomed the machinery of abandoned cranes. He stopped the car and we got out. I walked to the water: it looks greasy, heavy. A rope lay coiled nearby. Pieces of rusted metal open to the rain, curious relics gradually reducing to their mineral components. A Victorian brick warehouse behind.

Fell leaned against the car, watching me. I walked back towards him, holding my mouth still. As I came close I looked away, at the warehouse. He made a sudden movement, and my handbag dropped onto the ground, spilling open. I bent forward towards it. Fell gripped me by my arms and pulled me towards him. Off balance, I shifted and fell sideways onto the ground, he falling with me and with all his weight. Winded, I twisted and turned and sat up, knees folded up to my chest. We froze, staring at each other. I can feel redness coming up from my body. There is a smear of blood on his mouth.

He leaned his head back against the car, a little to one side. I moved forward until my face touched his. I tasted the red tepid saltiness of his gums, the smooth inside of his cheeks, the hard teeth. Our tongues locked and withdrew, probed and reconnoitred, silently. I can smell the oil and petrol of the car. The grit lying on the ground scrapes my legs.

His skin is softer than a man's should be ... I don't know why I should be surprised that there is no pain ...

Neither of us made a sound. His face lost all trace of expression.

DOUCEUR

ou manfuétude.

On perfonnifie la douceur par la figure d'une jeune fille aimable & gracieufe. Cette vertu qui eft
le principal mérite du beau fexe s'annonce par un
maintien modefte. L'olivier dont elle eft couronnée
étoit dédié par les anciens à la paix, & à Minerve
Déeffe de la Sageffe. L'éléphant lui eft donné pour
attribut à caufe de la bonté de fon cœur : l'agneau
pour la manfuétude dont il eft le fymbole, felon l'ap-
plication qu'en fait l'Ecriture ; & la colombe lui convient auffi, étant l'emblême fymbolique de la douceur.   L 5

GENTLENESS
or
COMPASSION

Gentleness is personified by the
figure of an amiable, gracious young
girl. This virtue, which is the principal merit of the fair sex, is shown by
a modest deportment. Her wreath is
of olive, dedicated by the Ancients to
peace, and to Minerva the Goddess
of Wisdom. The elephant is given as
an attribute of Gentleness because of
the kindness of its heart; the lamb
for the compassion which it symbol-
ises, according to the Scriptures; and
the dove is proper to Gentleness,
too, being its symbolic emblem.

It was a long time since the human noises in the house had quieted. Vira went out to the lights and voices of the street, which stayed alive longer. But she had to stop at the corner.

The old woman was lying flat on her back on the pavement.

- Are you all right? she asked.

The old woman said: Lovely night, isn't it?

She gave the impression of someone sunbathing, stretched out under artificial light.

- Shall I help you up?

- No, no, the old woman replied firmly. Don't worry about me. I'm fine.

How else should I react? A big, old woman lying in my path. Hard to ignore her.

Again the old woman said, Lovely night. This time she added, would you have a cigarette?

Vira interpreted this as a demand rather than an offer, and said she didn't have any. She suggested that she could go to the late-night super-market and buy some.

- No, no, said the old woman. You couldn't do that.

- O, I could, no problem. It's just down that road. I was going there anyway.

Under the blazing neon lights inside the shop, goods for sale were displayed in their start-lingly-coloured packages. A couple in leather jackets, with a white sports convertible outside the shop, had chosen this time to buy groceries. A drunk who only wanted rolling tobacco had to stumble all the way round the shop, bumping into the biscuit counter.

When Vira returned, the old woman had a pound note in her hand which she held straight up like a flagpole. Vira refused the money and handed over the cigarettes. The old woman found a box of matches under her clothing. Then she lit up in silence.

Will she drop ash on her face? I shall go, soon. Yes. Back to Dora's. What bad luck brings someone to this? The night never ends in the way you want. An hour ago, and now.

- I shall be going, now, Vira said.

- Bye, love, said the old woman.

Vira turned back onto the main street and past the late-night supermarket, round the block to resist insomnia, and into the narrow street from the other end. Two cats stood close together, bristling and screaming. One was black, the other the colour of the old woman's hair, a faint orange, and with the same small delicate nose. The black one pounced upon the other and rolled it into the dust, cuffing and biting.

Vira took out her key. As she went in through the door, the sandy cat was losing badly.

ICONOLOGIE

MENACE.

C'eſt la démonſtration extérieure qui ſert à intimi-
der par les actions ou par les paroles. On en
donne l'image par la figure d'une femme agitée, &
dont les yeux ſont ardents, & la face enflammée, ſui-
vant l'expreſſion d'Horace dans ſon Art poétique:

Iratum plena minarum.

Elle eſt en action de faire des reproches, & tient
une épée d'une main, & de l'autre un bâton, pour
faire la diſtinction par ces attributs des menaces faites
aux égaux, & de celles faites aux inférieurs.

Son vêtement eſt de couleur brune, & on la peint
dans une nuit non totalement obſcure, mais telle que
la peint Virgile Enéid. liv. 6.

Quale per incertam lunam ſub luce maligna
Eſt iter in ſylvis, ubi cælum condidit umbra
Jupiter &c.

THREAT

This is the external show which is
used to intimidate by word or deed.
It is figured as a perturbed woman
with blazing eyes and a glowing
face, after the expression of Horace
in his Poetic Art:
Iratum plena minarum.

She is in the act of upbraiding, and
holds a sword with one hand, and in
the other a cudgel, to make the
distinction between the attributes of
threats made to equals and those
made to inferiors.

Her garments are coloured brown,
and she is depicted before a night
sky which is not completely dark,
but rather such as the one in Virgil's
Aeneid, book 6:
*Quale per incertam lunam sub
    luce maligna
Est iter in sylvis, ubi caelum
    condidit umbra
Jupiter &c.*

There wasn't a sign at the door of the club. I've been to places like that. Only people who know about them can go. This one slightly worn like a leather jacket.

And I caught the reflection of blue in the corner of my eye. Marine blue, the colour of the deep sea, where the angler fish swim. The pressure down there is intense. If a fish is brought up to the top, it explodes.

But it's beautiful, too, marine blue. Underneath, there are colours you can't imagine, phosphorescent purples and greens and golds in the glow of the angler fish's lamp.

I was watching her as she came up. She knew how to walk like a woman, she knew how a woman was supposed to walk, and that was the way she did it. She must have practised. She didn't falter. The dress helped: marine blue. And her hair, like Greta Garbo's in *Flesh and the Devil*, slicked back, shoulder length. No cigarette, she wasn't an amateur. She wouldn't waste a gesture, she knew how much to give away. She wasn't young and innocent, she didn't waste a thing.

She came up and stood. She stood in front of me.

Standing is even more difficult than walking. She didn't stand with her legs slightly apart, or clasp her hands together, or put them on her hips. No handbag, no cigarette, no particular pose: the most difficult pose of all.

I had the sense that what she wanted was simply to hit me, the blow of blows, flat of hand to cheek, hard. Hard enough to knock me sideways. But it's not often a woman hits another woman, not in my experience.

Fell knows something that he didn't tell, that's clear. If she does hit me, it will be his fault. What is she to him?

She looked at me as if mentally she had finished a series of technical calculations. Her eyes gulped me down like a cold drink, painful at the base of the throat. And this at the moment when my own boundless jealousy and sense of inferiority began to make me admire her.

It's as if I've created this woman who, for all intents and purposes has no father or mother, no occupation, no proper name or age I see her existing in two kinds of places: near water, or in the bars and hotels and airports of international cities. I see her speaking any language she might choose. She doesn't sleep.

She asked me to dance. I went with her onto the dance floor. There were two boys dancing. Maybe they love each other. They were dancing apart, each self-absorbed in a choreography of golfing gestures. I was impressed.

We danced. We watched each other. We stopped dancing. We went into the bar and drank. That's her element, that's where she lives. If I wanted something else, I would have to make it happen myself.

I didn't want her to take me in her arms. The look of women is irresistible, beyond speech, but I don't like the feel of women's bodies. A man's body is simple. The softness of femininity, cushiony breasts, stomach, thighs. And I am like this, a sixteenth century Venus with a modern face. I didn't want something else, even if she did.

- You're leaving, she said.

- I hope I'll see you again.

- Yes, she said, and then: Perhaps.

But I didn't see her again.

FRANCOISE.

IMPRIMERIE.

Le blanc étant la couleur la plus pure, & la plus
fufceptible de l'impreffion des autres couleurs,
on l'a choifie pour celle du vêtement de cette figure; elle marque auffi que la qualité principale de
l'imprimerie eft d'être pure dans la correction. Sa
couronne eft de joubarbe, herbe qui refte toujours
verte. Elle tient une trompette avec ce mot: SEM-
PER UBIQUE, qui indique que par le fecours de
l'imprimerie les écrits des Savants fe répandent par
toute la terre. La caffette des lettres alphabétiques
& la preffe font des attributs qui s'expliquent
d'eux-mêmes.

PRINTING

White being the purest colour, and
the most susceptible to the printing
of other colours, it has been chosen
as that of the garments of this figure;
it also indicates that the most important quality of printing is to be pure
in its correction. The crown of the
figure is of houseleek, a plant which
is always green. She holds a trumpet
with these words: *Semper Ubique*,
which indicate that, with the aid of
printing, the writings of the Scholars
are spread all across the earth. The
case of letters of the alphabet and
the press are attributes which explain themselves.

He walked towards me. Although he saw me, his steps didn't quicken, but when he came close he touched me. I didn't shudder with desire. I hardly felt his touch at all.

I read in a French women's magazine that a man should have three attributes: Cheque, Chic et Chaud. Fell has all of them.

I was conscious of his corruption, which was the thing which drew me to him. There was something quite used in him, like a piece of paper which is crumpled and then smoothed out flat: he couldn't pass for new.

From the underground car park we took the lift to a floor near the top of the block. Of course I don't trust you. And at this moment I am closest to you.

I lay on the bed, face down. Fell stroked my back. He undressed and we moved under the bedclothes. There was no collision of flesh. The sheets were white. I slept.

I dreamt that I was falling asleep in a white bed. Fell was in the bed. In my dream, I fell asleep. As soon as I slept, Fell switched on a lamp next to the bed. He took a book from the bedside table and began to read. The book had a blank, white cover. He seemed to read, but I could see that each page was completely blank. I could also see myself asleep next to Fell. One odd detail was the chapter headings in Fell's blank book. Chapter One, Chapter Two. I could tell when Fell thought he was reaching the end of a chapter or beginning a new one.

Then, in my dream, he reached out to the same bedside table and there was a box of chocolates. It was a pale blue box and each chocolate was wrapped in gold paper with a blue band to match the box. I knew that the chocolates were poisoned. It was she who had done it. I'm afraid of being found out. I was afraid that he would die.

I woke sweating and crying. Fell was fast asleep beside me. Eventually, he woke up and tried to comfort me. I was inconsolable. He switched on the lamp by the bed. In its light I could see a box of chocolates, a black box, lying next to me on the bedside table. Black, not blue. My side, not his.

I fell asleep again. There were other dreams.

DEVINATION

ou divination du paganiſme.

Ciceron diſtingue deux ſortes de dévination, l'une de la nature, l'autre de l'art. A la premiere appartiennent les ſonges, & les idées ſuggérées à l'éſprit, ou les inſpirations naturelles, c'eſt ce qui ſe trouve annoncé par les différents oiſeaux qui entourent la tête de cette figure. A la ſeconde conviennent les augures, l'interprétation des oracles, la conſultation des entrailles des victimes, les étoiles, les foudres & autres ſuperſtitions.

On l'habille d'une eſpece de robe de prêtreſſe ornée de bandelettes, ſelon le rite des Egyptiens.

DIVINATION

Cicero distinguished two kinds of divination, one deriving from nature, the other from art. To the first belong dreams, ideas suggested to the mind, or natural inspirations, which are shown by the various birds around the head of this figure. To the second belong omens, the interpretation of oracles, the consulting of the entrails of victims, the stars, thunderbolts and other superstitions. The figure is dressed in a sort of priestess's robe trimmed with narrow bands, according with the rite of the Egyptians.

Vira had a preconceived formula for telling Dora about her move into Fell's flat. She would break the news plainly, but follow it with reasons and arguments.

She knew that Dora would not take her plans lightly. In fact she was secretly overjoyed, in advance, to think of causing her offence. She would be rupturing her carefully nurtured dependence on Dora. These feelings were mixed with apprehension. And just as Vira half expected, the scene did not go according to her blueprint.

She had the boxes of belongings removed already so that when it came to confronting Dora she could announce a fait accompli. She was very ill at ease, and could only just sit on the edge of the sofa facing her. Dora sipped tea from a white china cup, and, according to plan, Vira refused.

She ran through the explanations and arguments with a trickle of the gusto she had projected. She lacked the nerve, in the end, to affront Dora as she somehow wanted to. She floundered. And Dora was calmly examining the leaves of miniature palm in a pot with an expression of maternal solicitude. No trace of distress or discomposure.

Vira must have been unnerved. There was a silence. The silence lengthened. Her vital fluids ebbed. As she occasionally did in moments of distress, Vira looked from the window, but the beautiful trees in Dora's garden were bathed, shrouded in the evening fog.

This is not a warm country, and I have to cool even this warmth of Dora's, but it is a humid warmth. Because I have ambitions to be her, one day, to take her place.

Vira got up from the sofa and went over to the window, to pretend to observe the trees.

It was 'darling', finally as the tea-cup came quietly to rest on its saucer. Dora had never realised the full seriousness of Vira's involvement with Fell, she said. She should have, she said. Perhaps she had expected a little too much frankness? That was what she had come to expect from Vira.

- I haven't been deliberately secretive, Vira defended herself. It sounds just as if I am affirming the opposite. One can't deny things, with conviction.

Her face creased in premature defeat. The seams of her clothes rubbed against her skin. She waited.

- I only meant that, well, after all he isn't someone you've known long.

- No. What do you mean? That doesn't necessarily ....

- Not necessarily. But all the same.

- O God. You seem to want me to be so circumspect, Dora.

Vira blushed with repressed bad temper. Dora dislikes sloppiness in speech. I would never use the word 'circumspect' normally. I want to shout 'none of your bloody business'. But Dora isn't my mother.

At this point Vira walked back from the window to stand opposite Dora. By pure chance, she glanced into the teacup Dora had placed into its saucer. The tea-leaves made a shape like a scythe. This did not strike Vira as unlucky. She was not prepared to respond to this kind of phenomena and tended to regard people who did as weak-minded. She was wrong.

Dora poured some more tea into the cup and added milk.

- Isn't it stewed? Vira asked.

- Not at all.

- Where was it you first met Fell?

Dora bent her head to the cup, slightly. She has always been a good friend. What is it, what intimidates me?

- I'm not sure. Perhaps it was last year; yes, certainly it was last year.

- Perhaps it was at your other place.

Vira was smiling. Dora was smiling.

- I have a bad memory. I think you're right. It must have been there.

Dora continued to talk. Vira was thinking of the pointed corners of a mouth, of driving fast by the water, a smear of blood.

ICONOLOGIE

RICHESSE.

Aristophanes dans sa Comédie intitulée *Pluton*,
dépeint la richesse avec un bandeau sur les yeux.
Cet emblême signifie qu'elle ne va pas toujours cher-
cher le mérite. On la repréfente dans l'âge avancé,
parce qu'elle peut être le fruit d'une longue suite
de travaux, ou d'épargnes œconomiques. Sa comple-
xion maigre & son vêtement riche dénotent qu'elle
n'eft souvent qu'un contentement superficiel qui maf-
que des chagrins intérieurs. Son attribut ordinaire
eft une corne d'abondance dont elle verse des pieces de monnoye dans un vafe d'or.

WEALTH

In the Comedy entitled Pluto, Aristophanes depicts wealth with a blindfold over the eyes. This emblem signifies that wealth does not always seek merit. It is represented as a woman advanced in years, because it can be the fruit of a long succession of labours, or of sparing economies. Her drawn face and her rich clothing indicate that wealth is often only a superficial happiness which masks internal sorrows. The usual attribute of wealth is a horn of plenty from which she pours some coins into a gold vessel.

Fell drank straight from the neck of the bottle.
I was watching him pace back and forth on the
pebble beach. Half the bottle had gone already.

I was lying in a patch of sunshine, that day,
watching him. The wind was up. He didn't look
relaxed and happy, as he should have, as people
very often do, under similar circumstances. The
oblique sea-light darkened his dark hair and the
wind whitened his face.

His lips and teeth are stained red by the wine.

I could hear muttered words which blew towards me on gusts of wind:

- a crisis in international capital -

- unrealistic and utopian demands -

- free movement of labour -

- international market pressure -

From these clues I understood that Fell was
worried about his financial interests. In one of
the firms in which Fell had such interests, the
workers, teenage filipino girls, had gone on

strike against unsafe conditions and low pay. Most of Fell's investments were in this one firm. He had advised the other shareholders to give in to the girls' demands, which would anyway cost very little in terms of the total cost of producing the microelectronic components. A large profit could still be reaped, and especially if longer hours could be traded off for the extra safety and money which would be on offer. But one of the other shareholders, a military man who had not forgotten his days in Vietnam, had convinced the others that the strike was being orchestrated by dangerous subversive elements, linked to terrorist groups.

- Is the strike being orchestrated by dangerous terrorists? I shouted to Fell.

Then I turned over onto my stomach. Fell came to stand in front of me, a little grey in the face.

- You are going to lose all your money, I said.

- In the end, yes.

- No, now.

- Yes.

- Dora is rich. She might help you out.

- Might she?

- Yes.

- Maybe I'll speak to her.

I took the bottle from Fell, who sat down beside me in the sun. I drank some wine, gave the bottle back to Fell, and took a large bar of chocolate from my handbag. Fell refused the chocolate, so I ate the whole bar. I buried the silver foil and the wrapper under some pebbles.

Grey pebbles, dull, covered the beach. Fell and Vira were alone. Fell wore a dark suit, well-cut. He did not look English. He was tall, and muscular but not overtly so, just what we are supposed to like. And I do.

I do like the look of him: is that all that I like? No, it isn't quite all, but if it were all, it would be sufficient. I wouldn't demand anything else.

It is a bright, fresh day, clean as a watercolour. Red wine and chocolate, intermittent sunshine. But Fell thinks about imminent bankruptcy and

Vira … although everything is quite all right, so far …

ICONOLOGIE

REBELLION.

Cet excès populaire contre la difcipline, ou le gouvernement, s'exprime par une femme robufte, qui a le regard féroce, & la phyfionomie finiftre. Elle eft mal-vêtue, & armée en défordre. Le chat qu'elle a pour cimier à fon cafque, eft l'hiéroglyphe du peuple qui fupporte avec peine la fujétion & la contrainte. Elle tient une lance, une fronde, & fous fes piés font un joug brifé, un livre déchiré, & des balances rompues; ce qui fignifie que l'efprit de rebellion ne connoît ni raifon, ni loix, ni juftice.

REBELLION

This popular excess against discipline or the government is expressed here by a robust woman with a ferocious look and a sinister countenance. She is badly dressed and ill-armed. The cat on the crest of her helmet is the hieroglyph of the people, who can hardly bear subjection and constraint. She holds a lance and a sling, and under her foot is a broken yoke, a torn book, and a pair of broken scales; these signify that the spirit of rebellion knows neither reason, law nor justice.

Fell's bedroom, late morning, Vira lightly sleeping on the verge of wakefulness. Fell slipped out of the flat. Half an hour later, Vira got out of bed, went down in the lift and into the nearby café for breakfast. She noticed Fell sitting at one of the tables. Vira, feeling that today she looked a little like Anna Karina in *Vivre Sa Vie*, went over to him.

He was drinking coffee and there was a glass next to the coffee cup which contained a small pool of brandy. When he saw Vira he put out a cigarette. He was pallid and looked attractively unhealthy.

- How strange, said Vira. I've never seen you smoke before.

- I've only just started, said Fell. They make me feel rather sick, but I intend to persevere.

- What came in the mail? Vira wondered, before ordering herself a large breakfast.

- I feel faint with hunger, she said, falling upon the food.

-You are very scruffy, said Fell, looking at Vira's

unkempt hair and creased clothing. It is no use spending money on you. You don't appreciate it.

- That's true, said Vira. I'll pay for breakfast, if you like.

- The assembly base for microelectronic components is now all in little bits.

- O. Was it blown up by the extremists?

- One teenage saboteur and incendiarist. We weren't insured against sabotage.

Vira wiped her mouth with her napkin thoughtfully.

- How romantic! she said finally. What was she like?

- About fourteen years old, the average age of the girls there. Brought up by Roman Catholic nuns, and is still very devout.

- And what does she look like?

- Well apparently rather striking, in fact the

manager of the base had been trying to ... what does it matter, anyway? The point is that I'm bankrupt.

- She did it all on her own, this girl of fourteen?

- Yes.

- When I think what I was like at that age.

- They grow up more quickly in these third world countries.

- I don't suppose we're ever likely to meet her?

- I shouldn't think so.

- Will it be in the newspapers?

- Perhaps one or two.

- Perhaps I'll buy one today.

- What shall I do? said Fell, taking out a second cigarette.

LIBRE ARBITRE.

Saint Thomas, & Ariftote s'accordent fur la défi-
nition du libre arbitre, qui eft en nous la faculté
d'élire entre plufieurs chofes, celle qui femble de-
voir nous conduire à une fin. On le repréfente entre la jeuneffe & l'âge viril; fon vêtement royal,
fon fceptre & fa couronne défignent qu'il eft en
fa puiffance de vouloir ce qui lui plait; fon
manteau de diverfes couleurs fignifie l'incertitu-
de qui fe trouve fouvent dans le choix. La lettre
Y qui eft au haut de fon fceptre eft felon Pitha-
gore l'image de la vie humaine qui a un bon che-
min & un mauvis.

FREE WILL

Saint Thomas and Aristotle are in agreement on the definition of free will, which is our faculty to choose, among several things, the one which seems to lead to our purpose. It is represented as between youth and manhood; the man's royal garments, his sceptre and his crown signify that it is in his power to demand what he pleases; his cloak of many colours signifies the uncertainty which is often found in choice. The letter Y at the top of his sceptre is, according to Pythagoras, the image of a human life, which has one good way and one evil.

When the doorbell rang I sliced my leg. Just at the calf-bone, I sliced off a sliver. For a split second it went white: then a drop of blood formed. I ignored the doorbell and went on raking the razor up and down my leg. I wasn't expecting anyone, so I had no particular motive for getting out of the bath, except curiosity, and I was not, at that moment, curious. I was hoping that it wasn't someone connected to Fell's work.

The bell rang again. Completing the leg I hauled myself out and into a rough white bathtowel, and began to rub.

The bell rang a third time. I pulled on some clothes and went to the Ansafone. An identifiably male voice shouted 'Hello'. I pressed the button so that he could enter the main door.

It was the man with the principles about animals. I opened the door to let him in.

- Angel, this is the second time you have tried to cause a nasty accident. Thanks to you I will have a scab on my calf.

- We live in a fragile world. The balance could tip at any moment.

The man is obviously unusual, if not actually clinically insane.

- Well, if it did, most people wouldn't notice. If the balance did tip. Anyway, I don't know what you're talking about.

Angel's silence was broken only by a sneeze.

- Perhaps, I said finally, you would like a drink of some sort?

He accepted. I said to him that I could see there was something on his mind. Angel denied that anything was on his mind. He had a melancholy look which irritated me.

- What a mess, he remarked, looking around him at the slovenliness of the flat with the eagerness of a young child.

- It's nice, isn't it? I replied.

Angel went to look out of the window.

- Plane trees. I have terrible hay fever from plane trees.

- They are common around here, I said, pouring out two glasses of mineral water and holding one up for him.

- Your friend Dora, he said.

- Well, I suppose so, I said. I'm not absolutely certain.

- Said that, being short of money, you might be prepared to do some translation work. Angel finished the sentence in an exhausted voice. He drank half of the water and looked at the glass with no expression, which was his usual expression.

- I work in a museum, he continued after a pause. With a collection of old and rare books. He put up his hand to ward off some remark I was about to make. Please don't interrupt. We need a translation of some eighteenth century texts which accompany emblems; they are in French; I only read German. There's a fee attached, of course. Would you take it on?

Angel was rather white and on ending his speech, quickly drank the rest of the water and leaned back against the wall as if he might faint.

- Of course, I said. Are you all right?

- I feel rather weak.

Sometimes it is difficult to say one's lines.

- I can see you must find the administrative side of your work very taxing, I said.

He took out a thick hard-back book on whose spine was visible the words: *Boudard – Iconologie.*

- It's a facsimile reproduction, he said. I couldn't let you have the original.

LASSITUDE.

Ce fujet ne peut-être caractérifé que par l'abbattement des yeux, l'abandonnement du corps qui défigne la fatigue, & par la négligence dans les vêtemens. Le bâton fur lequel fe foutient cette figure indique le fecours néceffaire à la laffitude.

LASSITUDE

This subject can only be characterised by the drooping of the eyes, the
laxity of the body which shows
fatigue, and by the slovenliness of
the clothing. The stick with which
the figure supports herself indicates
the assistance needed for lassitude.

Vira lay on the sofa, prone and listless, her mental activity reduced to a minimum. When this happened, she became aware of the physical phenomena which surrounded her: the rain dripping unsteadily from an unfixed gutter-pipe; the sound of cars driving on wet tyres; the trees outside rustling. The reality of her environment impinged on her consciousness at such times: normally, she was hardly aware of it.

Nothing is ever good and wholesome. I wish I were someone else, somewhere else, not here and now and myself.

Occasionally, Vira flattered herself that she resembled slightly Anna Karina in *Vivre Sa Vie*, a film from the sixties about a glamorous prostitute who ends up murdered by gangsters. But at times like this Vira was aware that she didn't have the slightest resemblance to Anna Karina.

Rain dripped from the broken guttering. Vira swore to herself, trying to work up angry feelings. She sat up for a moment, but then slipped back to stare up at the bare, white ceiling.

The telephone rang. Vira picked up the receiver, listened for a moment, put it down again, and then unplugged it. She slipped back into a lizard-like stillness. Her eyes flickered at noises from the street. Several hours passed in this way.

While she lay looking up at the ceiling, the price of US dollars on the international money market changed minute by minute. Dealers were talking on several telephones at once in the money capitals of the world, buying and selling denominations. Several thousand babies were delivered and several thousand people met their death, peaceful or otherwise, during the hours of Vira's inertia, and the earth spun on its axis and continued its unending circling of the sun.

The earth spun on its axis.

Fell dozed in a hotel room, alone. The walls of the large room were painted white with a touch of grey. It overlooked, through a large window, a sumptuous bay whose deep blue waters gleamed with the reflected neon lights of hotel and restaurant signs, car headlights and street lamps.

He was lying with a thin sweat over his face, fully clothed, clumsily, in his dark business-man's suit and white shirt. His arms were crooked at each side of his face, as if to protect it from injury as he slept. Dream images - a golden casket filled with tiny snakes; a tunnel under the earth; a horse rearing in fright, bearing its big menacing teeth - came to his brain without forming a proper narrative, unsubstantial, half-grasped. He was dimly frustrated by this, by neither being quite asleep nor awake.

He stirred, then turned over onto his other side, and the motion of turning, or the cool sheet, unwarmed by body heart, which met his cheek, now caused a further stirring and a rousing of consciousness. He turned on his back, pushing out his legs in a sudden gesture, eyes squeezing open to two slits, then further, then blinking as his hands rubbed his face and pushed away the strands of hair which had fallen forward. He struggled to sit up, his legs over the edge of the bed, stayed like that for a moment, hands in hair, in a gesture which could be interpreted as despair, but was not, then got up and went to the bathroom.

The mirror told him that he needed a shave and that there were pink creases in his face from sleep.

He took off the suit and stood under the shower without drawing the shower curtain. The coolness of the water, which he let flow over him effortlessly, for minute after minute, calmed the race of alcohol in his blood. Wearily he rubbed soap into armpits and desultorily washed. As he stepped out of the shower, wrapped himself in the hotel's towel, stood dripping on the bathmat, the confusion of sleep and drink gave way to a sense of calm dereliction.

He shaved and dressed in a lighter suit, and as he combed his hair, the telephone rang. He picked up the receiver, listened, said 'Fine - I'll be down in half an hour -' returned it to the hook and took one last glance at the mirror, to straighten his tie.

Then he made his way down to the harbour. The others were waiting for him.

DIALECTIQUE.

C'eft l'art d'arranger fes idées pour raifonner jufte. On perfonnifie ce fujet par une femme coëffée d'un cafque , où font deux plumes, l'une blanche & l'autre noire, pour marquer que par la vigueur de l'intellect elle a la faculté de défendre avec des raifons probables le vrai comme le faux. Elle tient d'une main un eftoc qui a deux pointes de fer , & elle a l'autre main fermée. Ce gefte, felon Zénon, démontre la briéveté & la force de fes argumens.

DIALECTIC

This is the art of arranging one's ideas to reason soundly. The subject is personified by a woman wearing a helmet with two feathers, one white and the other black, to denote that through the vigour of the intellect she is able to defend through solid reasoning the false as well as the true. She holds in one hand a straight sword with two iron points, and her other hand is closed. This gesture according to Zenon, shows the brevity and force of her arguments.

Vira was working in the library, under the huge, domed roof. In another part of the library, people queued to look at the desk at which Karl Marx used to sit. Their eyes and hands rubbed along surfaces that his once had. The revolutionary, a communal memory, in which is invested some great love or hope, something that transcends the meagreness of using time.

Vira had only ever read *The Communist Manifesto* once, as a young girl, when she had a friend down the street who was in the Party. But that didn't prevent her from participating in this nostalgia for the great man's vision, or what little she knew of it.

Vira took out a notepad and began to write. Then with an exasperated expression, she put down the pen and searched through her case, finally drawing out a new pen with which she went back to writing. She was anxious, with an habitual anxiety, about beginning. Paralysis seemed to her a more natural state than activity. But still, eventually, a tiny movement was made, the hand across the page, for a series of moments, words were formed. She wrote as if she were murmuring to herself, aloud:

Slow afternoons recoiling slowly into evening

Evening retreats

Night is the join between days, we should not know the join

She thought: The sky covers the earth as a dome which stretches beyond the eye's capacity. The place of prognostications and gaseous clouds, God's wrath. In the Middle Ages God watched us from the sky, from up there, in the highest heaven, the Heaven of Heavens.

The sky, observed in its minutiae by scholarly scientists, astronomers. Observed and quantified and occasionally rockets sent into its depths, fireworks which bang and fizzle and are over quickly. Can anyone imagine even one single light year? It will take millennia to make the vastness of space thinkable. Can we really imagine what forever means?

Slow afternoons recoiling slowly into evening

White days, a quarter through the year, dull days of anxious half-thoughts, bent over books or gazing at the nib of a pen

Vira paused. She bit her thumb. She listened to

the noises around her. A rustling of pages, a setting down of books, the squeak of a door, a cough, the sound of someone walking. She turned to a thick volume lying in front of her, Boudard's *Iconologie*, a facsimile reproduction of a eighteenth century dictionary of moral emblems. She opened it at random, scrutinising an image of a woman with two feathers sprouting from her head, one black and the other white. The emblem was named 'Dialectique'. She began to work.

ICONOLOGIE

MORT.

Ordinairement on la peint en fquélette, ayant
des ailes, une faux, & un horloge à fable.
Outre que cette image eſt affreuſe & trop ordinaire,
il eſt mieux de la repréſenter fous la figure d'une
femme pâle, avec un bandeau fur les yeux, deux
grandes ailes, & une draperie noire· Elle tient une
faux & un crochet: ce dernier attribut eſt tiré du
Prophete Amos:

Uncinum pomorum ego video.

Et tous les deux fignifient que fon empire s'étend
fur les derniers, comme fur les premiers des hom-
mes. Ce qui eſt encore autoriſé par cette ſentence
d'Horace. *liv.* i. od. 4.

Pallida mors æquo pulſat pede pauperum tabernas,
Regumque turres.

Lib. i. od. 23.

Miſta ſenum ac juvenum denſantur funera. Nullum
Sæva caput Proſerpina fugit.

ME-

DEATH

Ordinarily it is portrayed as a skeleton, having wings, a scythe and an hourglass. As this image is hideous and too commonplace, it is better to represent it by the figure of a pale woman, with a blindfold over her eyes, two great wings, and black draperies. She holds a scythe and a crook: this last attribute is taken from the prophet Amos:

Uncinum pomorum ego video.
And these two things signify that death's empire extends to include the last men on earth, as it included the first. This is also authorised by Horace, book 1, ode 4.

Pallida mors aequo pulsat pede
pauperum tabernas,
Regumque turres.

Book 1, ode 23
Mista senum ac juvenum densantur
funera. Nullum
Saeva saput Proserpina fugit.

It was too late to go into the church. The service had already started. I could hear the choir singing 'Ave Maria'. I stood anxiously in the porch, anxious and yet unable to disguise from myself feelings of intense pleasure at the memories that the place evoked. There were marble fingerbowls, but I did not dip my fingers and make the sign of the cross. I remembered the medieval church in Brittany where I had seen, painted on the walls inside, on the whitewashed stone walls, the living and the dead join together in a danse macabre. Rich merchants and their plump wives hand in hand with skeletons; riotous, courtly, decorous and intimate.

A fleshless arm flailing upwards to the roof. A plump knee nudging an outthrown leg-bone. The living losing themselves in reckless sensuality with the dead, rosy lips pouting at laughing eye sockets, covert vows made across the flickering candlelight as they whirl round and round.

I went out of the church and into the graveyard which covered a short slope at the back of the church. I still felt the odd exhilaration that the moments in the church had brought. Partly from the memory of the danse macabre, and also because of other memory traces, so many as to be unspecific, to form a kind of mental texture, a sort of uneasy familiarity which still resonated with the incomprehension and blurred impressionability of childhood.

I walked between the white marble plaques and graves covered with green stones, and it seemed that above my head the clouds moved more quickly and the shadows of the clouds distinctly passed over the earth. I stood for a moment against a monument and looked back towards the church. I waited for someone to come out. But this waiting reminded me of something else, something difficult to describe: a sense of loss absolutely agonising, a longing, unbearably sweet, without reason, like being hopelessly in love.

Standing in the graveyard I remembered the time in Brittany, and saw the painted figures of danse macabre on the stone walls of the church. And this time will never come back to me, these days are gone as if I watched them on a cinema screen, except that there are no copies, there is no repeating, no holding of anything, nothing but this movement forward, forward.

I caught sight of Dora as she moved through the tombstones towards me, and saw that behind her the congregation was leaving: the mass was over. She was coming towards me with a half-smile, a smile which implied love, and the pain of some suppression, bending her face a little as if careful of her step. Then she looked up.

I smiled at once, and asked her how she was. She told me that she had been very busy. She said that she was sorry about Fell. She said she hadn't been able to say so before now. So now she wanted to say it.

- You didn't like him much, did you? I said.

- He was just what you wanted at the time, she said.

- We are getting on better, these days, I said. I wanted to see you again. But I suppose you're busy.

- I have to go. But come to the house tomorrow.

I walked with her to her car, and waved as she drove away.

INFIRMITE.

On la peint fous la figure d'une vieille femme, pâle & exténuée. Elle eft affife dans un fauteuil, foutenant d'une main fa tête, tenant de l'autre une branche d'anémones fauvages. Les anciens fe fervoient de cette fleur en médecine; & chez les Egyptiens elle étoit l'hiéroglyphe de la maladie; c'eft pourquoi on en fait l'attribut de ce fujet.

INFIRMITY

It is portrayed by the figure of an old woman, pale and drawn. She sits in an armchair, one hand supporting her head, the other holding a sprig of wild anemones. The Ancients used this flower in medicine; for the Egyptians it was the symbol of illness; that is why it is made the attribute of this subject.

The old woman, built big and square like a barn, lay face-down on a carpet which once had some sort of pattern. It was early in the morning, around six.

I walked in and circled, then noticed the dark viscous trail from nostrils and mouth: blood. I heaved her onto her back. The nose had been smashed. I began to cry. The tears continued to fall from my eyes for as long as I remained with her.

I ran cold water onto a greyish-white flannel of Chinese origin, and dabbed at the old face, perhaps too timidly. The blood stuck, a tacky membrane over the lower part of her face.

She made a sort of snorting noise. Her eyes were open but devoid of lambency. When I moved my hand in front of them, they didn't respond. If I put my face straight in front of her, she appeared, uncannily, to see me.

- Comatose, I muttered aloud like a gifted neurologist.

Oddly, although there was hardly any furniture in the place, there was a telephone. I called 999 and asked for an ambulance: one would arrive in a quarter of an hour.

She made a noise as if she were being throttled. I ignored this for the moment and took out a handkerchief to wipe some of the salt water from my sweater, which was soaked with tears.

I went into the kitchenette and switched on the electric kettle. It immediately wheezed strongly. I pulled out the plug and put some water into it, to silence the wheezing. When it boiled, I damped the little Chinese flannel and wrung it out. Going over to her I rubbed vigorously, abrasively even, at the blood. It came off in small pieces. The old woman, always so grim-faced, looked straight ahead of her with a mild expression. She made another noise, this time as if she were snoring. These noises that she made were both reassuring and worrying - they proved that she was actually still alive but implied that it wouldn't be for long.

I wonder why, today of all days, she decided to put on a lemon-yellow twinset over a nylon patterned dress. Her bust, stately like the prow of a ship, was soiled from contact with the floor. I went behind her and with some difficulty, tugging from her armpits, hauled her onto the bed. She was rather cold to the touch. I piled on blankets, tucked her in carefully, and arranged her hair skilfully on the pillow, to make a more attractive and bearable sight.

The old woman is ill, I could now say to myself. She looks awful. I hope she'll be all right. The tears stopped for the duration of these mental phrases and then started flowing again immediately, owing to their feebleness and poverty. The whole of the upper front of my sweater was soaked.

Standing by the window I watched a young blonde woman in a short leather coat and stilettos push a toddler in his pushchair. He was dirty and blank; must have been conceived when she was thirteen. She looked immaculate.

It's quiet in here. Outside, most of the houses look abandoned. Probably everyone except the old woman accepted rehousing in one of those tower blocks.

The ambulance arrived and the men slid her into the back like a slice of cake onto a plate.

- I hardly know her at all, I repeated to the men. They largely ignored me.

My tears stopped as the ambulance moved off down the street. Poor old woman, I said to myself. I hope she will be all right. I walked out of the house and out of the street and out of the neighbourhood. It was easy.

My hands were in my pockets. Anything is happening and will continue to happen, with or without my consent. I only exist as a flickering image with a limited screen time.

I C O N O L O G I E.

C'eſt le nom de la Science contenue dans ce livre, elle fait diſtinguer les attributs, les ſymboles, & les Hiéroglyphes dont on ſe ſert pour caractériſer les Vertus, les Vices, & toutes les Paſſions que l'on veut perſonnifier. Les Egyptiens en ayant été les premiers inventeurs, on la repréſente vêtue & coëffée à l'Egyptienne, tenant d'une main une plume & de l'autre un peinceau d'où partent des traits qui ſemblent animer des génies qui ſont près d'elle. Le diſtinctif de ſes génies eſt une petite flamme qu'ils ont ſur la tête, & les attributs qu'ils tiennent déſignent quels vices ou quelles vertus ils repréſentent.

ICONOLOGY

This is the name of the Science
contained in this book, which is able
to distinguish the attributes, the
symbols and the Hieroglyphs that
are used to characterise the Virtues,
the Vices and all the Passions one
wants to personify. Because the
Egyptians were the first inventors of
it, Iconology is shown as a woman
with clothing and hair in the Egyp-
tian style, holding a pen in one hand
and in the other a paintbrush from
which come rays which seem to
animate the spirits which are near to
her. What marks these spirits is a
small flame that they each have on
their head, and the attributes they
hold designate which vices or virtues
they represent.

Angel called on Vira to collect the typed translations of the texts from the book he had given her.

Vira had been intrigued by the unusual book, but also a little baffled, and irritated. She asked him to explain something about it.

Angel: The emblems are concepts translated into images. They were meant to be completely conventional, so that anyone with any education could understand them.

Vira: I suppose that everyone had to be able to read back from the visual to the linguistic -

Angel: Well, there was always a text underneath so that wasn't too difficult.

Vira: But the emblem had to rely on the received notion of any concept it represented - a consensus definition. So it was like an early attempt to impose certain ways of thinking.

Angel: I'm not sure about that. The main basis of the whole thing was metaphor. Abstract concepts have always been difficult to grasp, and metaphors were used to make them easier to understand. Many of these metaphors were drawn from the realm of sight - 'the darkness of ignorance' and so on. So it wasn't really so surprising that finally someone would come along and try to make a system of realised visual emblems representing such concepts.

Vira: But this system had to exclude other metaphors, I suppose, which might have existed or come into being to try to make other conceptualisations of things like friendship, death, and so on.

Angel: That's not what Ripa and his followers, including Boudard, thought. Ripa, the first one to make a book like this of emblems, was an amateur Aristotelian. Aristotle thought that all words were names of things or people, language was literal and offered a total inventory of reality. So that metaphor wasn't a means of conceptualising, but simply an enjoyable form which could always, ultimately, be dispensed with. Aristotle worked by thinking about the qualities and properties of concepts and thus defining them.

Ripa followed Aristotle by looking for material objects which shared the same properties as the concept, then illustrating them. Take the concept 'Fortune', for instance. Its property is that it can't be grasped, it doesn't stay in one place, with one person, but constantly moves on. Ripa would illustrate Fortune by a wheel, which also moves constantly.

Vira: But isn't a metaphor something which creates meaning, rather than illustrating it? And in any case, the translation of a linguistic metaphor into a visual emblem is fraught with dangers. Looking at these emblems, it's not at all obvious, without the text at any rate, to what they refer. Instead of being easily accessible, as they were meant to be, they seem to produce bafflement. You're left wondering what on earth an olive branch means when set next to a dead rabbit and an open compass.

Angel: I don't remember that one -

Vira: I was only making it up, but do you see what I mean? Perhaps all it comes down to is that Aristotle was the first victim of a passion for classification and systematisation. He first practised on animals, didn't he?

Angel: Yes. The basis of Aristotelian definition was the classification and subdivision of the animal kingdom.

133

Vira: And wasn't he the one to call man the 'rational animal'?

Angel: Mm. If you're really interested, I could ...

Vira: I just thought what an odd thing, because animals are dumb, and can't let us into their perceptions, if they have any, and so we can't really know anything about them, ultimately, we couldn't know the most important things. Which seems a very odd basis for the origins of logic and rationalism, don't you think?

Angel: Well, I don't quite see ... I don't suppose that it matters very much to a vole that it's generally known as a vole and not a mole, or a caterpillar, or for that matter -

Vira: A hedgehog?

Angel: As you say. But to come back to the emblems, for me the thing I like about them, I do like them very much, is that they are not quite as straightforward as they try to claim to be. Humans with wings on their shoulders or feet, or both; people with animals or bizarre instruments perched upon their head or held in the hand; very strange.

134

Vira: That's true.

Angel: They remind me of dream-images, condensed and displaced from their original meaning, and which need the key of language to be understood. These hybrid compositions, almost all menacing or disquieting, don't seem to either deny or reflect our waking perceptions, but to rearrange them in a way which is supposed to be systematic, but suggests more of the distortion and perversity of the unconscious.

Vira: I didn't suspect you of these kinds of ideas, Angel.

Angel: It's as if the moment of enforcing meanings brings back the most ambiguous things to the surface of the image. It's as you said about Aristotle: a system for defining what ultimately can never be understood.

Vira: Angel, I am not quite sure what you mean.

Angel: Well, sometimes, someone whose job it is to organise and systematise things, like me, who works in a museum, likes to think that some things always escape, even that everything always escapes.

135

Vira: That reminds me of when I was a little girl: I used to think that my toys came awake at night and danced around. But I never saw them, although I always wanted to.

Angel: It never disturbed your faith when every morning the toys would be back in the exact same position in which you had put them to bed the previous night?

Vira: No. That didn't worry me at all.

FRANÇOISE.

TRAHISON.

Cet infame excès, qui deshonnore l'humanité, eſt perſonnifié par une vieille femme d'aſpect affreux, qui careſſe un jeune adoleſcent, & qui dans le même tems qu'elle lui donne un baiſer, ſe prépare à lui donner un coup de poignard.

BETRAYAL

This vile excess, which dishonours
humanity, is personified by an old
woman with a terrible look, who
caresses a youth, and at the same
time as kissing him, prepares to stab
him with a dagger.

- Fell's landlord has given me three weeks to vacate the flat. I can't afford the rent, which is astronomical.

- Did that man I met the other day ever get in touch with you?

- Mm? So I have to look for another place. It's not going to be easy.

- The one you almost crashed into, on the road. You remember. You were sick.

- O yes, that one. Yes, he did. Angel, you mean. I've been working a lot for him to pay for a pair of shoes I found, dark green suede with yellow furry giant bees attached. You'd like them. They were very expensive.

- I'm not sure that I would like them. In fact, they sound terrible.

- Why? Nobody thought any the worse of Elsa Schiaparelli for making shoe-shaped hats, or tailored suits with lips for pockets.

- Schiaparelli was an artist. That is quite different.

141

Dora and I were lying in canvas deck chairs in her garden. Huge, shameless roses exuded their exquisite fragrance into the air. I was wearing a pair of shorts. Dora wore a floral dress and displayed unexpectedly perfect, slightly speckled brown feet.

- Well, if anyone mentions anything ...

- I'm afraid that seems unlikely, Vira.

I looked round sharply at Dora.

- The perfume of these roses ...

She was gazing thoughtfully at nothing in particular.

- Yes, it is lovely.

I waited for a moment, then went on.

- So you think it's unlikely you will hear of anything, Dora.

She looked at me, smiling slightly.

- You look so well now, Vira. You seem to have completely got over your depression about Fell.

- It's odd. I'm not sure about 'getting over'. But it's true that I feel much better.

- You see, Vira, over and above everything, Fell is a businessman. Rather a successful one, until recently.

- I never really saw that side of him.

- I know you didn't. He didn't want you to see it. He half-pretended not to see it himself. But now he's had to give up those illusions. That's why he left Europe.

.

I didn't say anything immediately. I was wondering why Dora was telling me all this. Was she demanding some special privilege? I couldn't guess what.

- I'm not sure if 'business' doesn't require a particularly developed capacity for illusion, I said finally. But I should remember that you, too, Dora are a businesswoman.

- There's something else, Dora said.

I kept picking idly at the lawn. She watched me.

- Go on.

- I shall be leaving here in a few days - next Thursday. I'm going to Tokyo.

I straightened up to look at her.

- That's a long way, I said non-committally. You might want to visit Fell, if he's still there.

- Yes, I shall be going to see him. In fact, I shall be seeing quite a lot of him, she said in a toneless voice.

- There's obviously something I don't understand, I said, similarly without expression.

- Something I haven't been ready to mention before now. Or that you weren't ready for. Fell is working for me. The group of companies I own is expanding into Japan. With his contacts and experience, Fell was an obvious choice for our front runner.

- Fell works for you? Front runner. What's that? He's your employee? You're his boss?

- He now has a number of shares, so it's not quite like that. But on the whole, you're quite right.

- How lucky for you, Dora. It's hardly possible for me to believe this. It seems, then, that it must have been on your very own suggestion that Fell disappeared: in pursuit of your 'business' interests.

- As you say, I merely made the suggestion. He accepted with alacrity. It was a very good opportunity for him.

- A good opportunity, I repeated. And why didn't you tell me all this before?

She leaned back in her chair, folding her hands behind her head.

- Isn't that obvious? You were hardly in the right frame of mind. But I knew you would come through. You have come through. I was waiting for the right moment. Now was the right moment.

- I never suspected anything like this. I always thought it was his decision. But it was yours -

- It wasn't mine. It was his. Don't jump to the wrong conclusion, Vira. It wasn't as you think.

- It wasn't as I think. What do you mean? What do you think I'm thinking? What does that mean?

Her nostrils dilating slightly.

- How was it, exactly, Dora?

I stood up and walked down the length of the garden and back to stand in front of Dora.

- For a moment I wondered, when you said you'd met him in the country. I thought it then. But after a while I couldn't believe it. I forgot it. I thought it was probably all over, if it had ever happened. I was living with him. I thought I would have noticed if anything was wrong.

- I don't think you -

- No, listen, wait. Tell me how I couldn't have known. Tell me how it was that I never knew, until now.

Dora, looking down at the ground, looked up

savagely and said in a grating voice, I suppose
you assumed that I was too old.

- Tell me a bit more, Dora. I think I should know
a little bit more. Take me through it: explain.

- It's not so easy. You and I had been close, I felt
that, a sort of closeness, quite different from ...
until you began to see him. It immediately
changed you, you seemed to come to resent me
in some way. It was obvious you were nothing
to him. I couldn't stand you wanting so much to
be this nothing. I thought about it a lot. It
seemed purely ... self-destructive ... on your
part.

At this point I was close to tears. Dora was
betraying me again, pretending not to know my
real feelings.

- You mean you could see very easily what I saw
in him.

- Very well, said Dora scornfully. Have it as you
will. I wanted what you had.

I felt completely distracted, unable either to
defend or attack.

147

- I won't go into detail, she said.

- I've had enough, in any case, I said.

I could hardly move my lips.

TRANQUILLITÉ.

On la repréſente aſſiſe paiſiblement, & regardant une mer en calme. Son ſymbole eſt un Alcyon dans ſon nid. Cet oiſeau a le plumage bleu, vert & rouge, & le bec tranchant. Les anciens le conſideroient comme le précurſeur du beau tems.

Voyez dans les Métamorph. d'Ovide liv. 11. ce qu'il dit de l'Alçyon :

Perque dies placidos hyberno tempore ſeptem
Incubat halcyone pendentibus æquore nidis.
Tum via tuta maris : ventos cuſtodit, & arcet
Æolus egreſſu : præſtatque nepotibus æquor.
Hos aliquis ſenior circum freta lata volantes
Spectat : & ad finem ſervatos laudat amores.

QUIET

This is represented as a figure sitting
peacefully, watching a calm sea. Its
symbol is a Kingfisher in its nest.
This bird has blue, green and red
plumage, and a sharp beak. The
ancients regarded it a harbinger of
good weather.
Consider in Ovid's Metamorphoses,
book II, what he says of the kingfisher:

> Perque dies placidos hyberno
>   tempore septem,
> Incubat halcyone pendentibus
>   aequore nidis.
> Tum via tuta maris: ventos
>   custodit et arcet
> Aeolus egressu: praestatque
>   nepotibus aequor.
> Hos aliquis senior circum freta
>   lata volantes
> Spectat: et ad finem servatos
>   laudat amores.

151

The old woman's eyes were bright and the purple bruising which I had last seen dominating her face had faded to a relatively acceptable yellow. She sat up in bed brightly and the young nurse remarked how 'lively' she was looking today, as she inserted our sheaf of freesias into a vase.

- They won't last long in here, she said. Too bloody hot. Like a greenhouse.

- Wouldn't want you to catch cold, said the nurse, smiling and leaving.

- Why not? said the old woman, although the nurse was now out of earshot.

She turned to us.

- More work for them, I suppose. They prefer the cleaning aspect of the job.

- I brought someone to see you, I said. This is Angel, a new friend of mine.

Angel seemed amused and acutely nervous. I was pleased to notice that his reaction to the old woman was similar to mine.

- Angel once nearly killed me. By accident, in a car.

- A car accident? she said.

Angel said that he had to go soon, to be on time for something. As he was leaving the ward, the old woman leaned forward in a confidential way.

- I didn't like to say anything while your boyfriend was here, she said, loudly, but do I know you?

I reminded her that I had gone to buy cigarettes for her once, and that we had encountered one another on several occasions since then. I told her my name.

- Ah, she said, leaning back on her pillows. She seemed satisfied that a connection had been established.

After some time I mentioned our last encounter, when I had come to her home and found her in the condition which had required her immediate hospitalisation.

She objected to the word hospitalisation; and said that she was not at all sure that in any case it had been necessary. She was sure, in fact, that she would have been all right eventually. I thought of asking her about how she had come to be in such a condition in the first place, but thought better of such an enquiry. She seemed to have no interest in satisfying any curiosity I might feel.

I was curious, but at the same time I felt that the truth might disturb me. My equilibrium was fragile, and I couldn't face any sort of challenge.

Changing the subject, I told her that she had been investigated by the social services, and from now on would be visited by a home help and a meals on wheels service. She heard me out in silence.

- They like to clean up, she said finally. I've never been one for it myself.

The squalor of her living quarters certainly testified to this.

- Perhaps it won't be so bad, I suggested. She said nothing for a moment, then:

- They swab me all over with a sponge in bed.

- How do you feel about that? I asked anxiously.

- I don't know, she said firmly. I don't know how I feel.

FRANÇOISE.

FIN.

Ce nom fignifie plufieurs chofes; mais principalement la fin de toute chofe. C'eft dans ce fens que Petrarque a dit:

Quefte cofe, che 'l Ciel volge, e governa,
Dopo molto voltar, che fine avranno?

Le même auteur l'adaptant à la mort, qui eft la fin de tout ce qui vit, dit:

Signor della mia fine, e della vita.

On perfonnifie ce fujet par un vieillard, qui a la barbe blanche & la tête chauve; il eft couronné de lierre, plante qui détruit les édifices où elle s'attache. Son vêtement eft de couleur feuille-morte: il regarde triftement la terre, tient un livre fermé où eft l'omega grec. Derriere lui eft un Soleil couchant.

END

This name signifies several things: but principally the end of everything. It is in this sense that Petrarch has said:

Queste cose, che 'l Ciel volge, o
  governa,
Dopo molto voltar, che fine
  avranno?

The same author, applying the word to death, which is the end of all that lives, says:

Signor della mia fine, e della vita.

The subject is personified by an old man with a white beard and a bald head; he is crowned with ivy, a plant which destroys buildings to which it attaches itself. His clothing is russet, the colour of dead leaves: he looks sadly at the earth and holds a closed book showing the Greek letter omega.
Behind him is the setting Sun.

Vira stood on the shore, watching the sea moving towards and away from her. A bird flew over the beach, calling loudly. Vira turned her head to follow its flight.

The bird flew over the beach.

The tide moved forward, then receded.

Vira stood watching.

When the bird was out of sight she began walking along the shore.

161